THE

HAUNTED BOOKSHELF

he telling or reading of ghost stories during long, dark, and cold Christmas nights is a yuletide ritual dating back to at least the eighteenth century, and was once as much a part of Christmas tradition as decorating fir trees, feasting on goose, and the singing of carols. During the Victorian era many magazines printed ghost stories specifically for the Christmas season. These "winter tales" didn't necessarily explore Christmas themes. Rather, they were offered as an eerie pleasure to be enjoyed on Christmas Eve with the family, adding a supernatural shiver to the seasonal chill.

The tradition remained strong in the British Isles (and her colonies) throughout much of the twentieth century, though in recent years it has been on the wane. Certainly, few people in Canada or the United States seem to know about it any longer. This series of small books seeks to rectify this, to revive a charming custom for the long, dark nights we all know so well here at Christmastime.

THE HAUNTED BOOKSHELF

THE HAUNTED BOOKSHELF

THE HOUSE BY
THE POPPY FIELD

THE HOUSE BY THE POPPY FIELD

MARJORIE BOWEN

A GHOST STORY FOR CHRISTMAS

DESIGNED & DECORATED BY SETH

BIBLIOASIS

HEN MAITLAND FIRST saw the house the poppies were in full bloom; he had never before seen so many blooming together; the field was a sheet of scarlet flecked with green, right up to the hedge of unclipped yew that divided the garden from the pasture land; also large mauve poppies with a deep stain at the base of each petal rose from the long parterres at the side of the lawn; the property was in tolerable condition but had the melancholy air of a place for long not lived in and only superficially cared for by tired indifferent hands.

Maitland had inherited Bothal from a distant relative who for years had left the estate in the charge of an estate agent and a caretaker, and Maitland now past middle age had himself lived a wandering eccentric life; a solitary man, therefore, gazed at a solitary house; a shade passed over his lined face, cast by the cloud that sailed over the poppy field and gave a darker hue to the waving flowers.

Bothal, built in a Jacobean Baroque style, had three ornate gables, in each of which was set a classic bust of yellow stone; the windows were handsomely finished with stone facings that showed richly against the warm purplish pink of the bricks; round the lower windows and over the white classic porch grew a tangle of small shell-tinted roses; the cloud passed and the sun was brightly over the empty house, the poppy field, the garden where Maitland stood alone.

As he gazed at the roses against the brick, the blank windows, the closed door, an unutterable nostalgia shook him; what was he regretting, what seeking?

He had pursued his chimera in many parts of the world and never felt so near her hidden presence as now; he glanced at the keys in his hand; "Of course I shall sell," he had told the agent, "the place is much too large and uncouth for me."

And for most people, the agent had hinted; Bothal had been untouched for a good many years, it was not, in any sense of the word, modernized—a desirable, but not a saleable property, though a pretty piece of period architecture, the man of business had said.

Maitland passed under the porch; again the shadow glided over the poppy field, the house, again the cloud passed rapidly and the sun again drew up the hot scent of the box hedge.

The new owner turned the key and entered his mansion; his ancestors had lived there, generation after generation, long before, but Maitland had no sense of coming home; everything seemed strange, yet he was filled by an inexplicable yearning.

Everything within the house was swept and dusted, but this neatness seemed only to accentuate the desolation; the place had not the air of being left to gradual ruin, but rather appeared as if it were being kept trim for someone who would never return, or was very long away. This sad expectancy had to Maitland a deeper sadness than the utter abandonment of hope. The walls of the first room that he entered were, in the fashion of a bygone day, stretched with canvas that was painted with sombre landscapes of purple rocks, shadowed streams, storms blowing up against lonely places and plains strewn with broken pillars. Maitland opened the shutters; as the sunshine streamed into the loneliness, he winced.

"People should not leave houses standing when they no longer intend living in them," he muttered to himself. "No, every house that is not inhabited should be pulled down."

Yet he would not have said that the place was haunted; it seemed, indeed, intolerably empty even of ghosts; it was that air of waiting that Maitland found so unendurable—waiting for what, for whom? He walked through all the rooms on the ground floor; they were clean and the house had been kept well repaired; there were no marks of damp or rats, of spiders or decay; the window panes were bright

and here and there were some pieces of furniture, a settee covered in red rep, a pair of embroidered chairs protected by canvas covers, a glass-fronted case in which stood rows of leather-backed, polished books, a table or two, a couple of andirons in front of the marble mantlepiece—all as if someone had moved out yesterday or was moving in tomorrow. Maitland went upstairs to the top of the house; in the front was a long gallery, with a sloping floor, and a dais for musicians; this was completely bare; the walls had been painted, on the plaster, with an Italian scene, now utterly faded; only here and there could be discerned the misty azure of a mountain or a lake; the windows were those of the gables; they had deep box seats of mellow coloured wood and were unshuttered, through them streamed the sunlight, yellow and rich as rum honey; Maitland felt that if he put his fingers in it and then tasted them, he would savour the sweetness of the entire summer; the back of the house was divided into two large bedrooms; in each was an old-fashioned bed with mattress, tester and coverlet in good repair; the curtains, of thick woollen material strewn with balls of camphor, were lying on the beds.

Maitland opened the window in the slightly large room; he looked onto the field of poppies that encircled the house at the back; here the boundaries of the garden had been broken down and the wild flowers had flowed into what had been the lawn; Maitland thought that he could detect a perfume, like the acrid whiff of a narcotic, on the air.

He thought, "Why should I not stay here for a while? There is nothing for me to do, no one waiting for me."

It seemed as if a voice breathed over his

shoulder—"no one?" with that rise at the end of the sentence that means a question.

Maitland turned and looked about the room, so neat, so clean, so empty; he felt a mingling of the eternal pangs that torment humanity—a nostalgia for a lost childhood, a yearning to escape life through death, the eager desire for the dreamless sleep.

"Why not stay?" he mused. "Here one could collect one's thoughts, perhaps write some of them down,—perhaps—who knows?—find a clue to the meaning of some of it."

He left the house doors and windows open to the sunlight and went to the lodge at the other end of the park, where the caretaker and his wife lived; after complimenting them on the good condition of Bothal, he told them of his intention of staying there a few days and they came back with him, bringing a few necessaries, bed linen, blankets, a lamp, candles and cutlery; Maitland then asked the man to go down to the inn and order his sparse luggage to be sent up to Bothal.

A few adjustments soon made the bedroom habitable; there was water to be obtained by using a pump in the kitchen, for the rest of Bothal was without "conveniences."

"Old-fashioned, as you might say," apologized the caretaker; "but there, no one has lived in the house for so long, and all say it would cost more than the place is worth to put in improvements, though I say that you'd hardly know it with electric light and steam heating, not to mention bathrooms and a telephone."

"A wonder," remarked Maitland, "that it hasn't by now, got the reputation of being haunted—but you have kept it very neat and clean and let in the light every day."

"We've done our best, sir. I won't say but that the garden has got out of hand—it would take more than the labour that we're allowed to keep all that land in order."

"The poppies," smiled Maitland. "They have rather overrun the place."

"I've never seen so many of them as there are this year."

"And you've never heard of any ghost stories? They are usual in a place like this."

The caretaker's wife answered cheerfully.

"There was an old man who used to work in the garden when we first came, sir, he said there were tales of the shade of a little black boy that used to haunt the long gallery—but we've never seen nor heard anything, and I don't, for my part, think that the old fellow knew what he was talking about."

"Quite likely. I see there are no portraits in the place—no personal relics."

"No, sir, old Mr Maitland used to come on rare occasions, sir, in a big grey car, and take away all the pictures, and things like that."

"Do you remember any of them? The pictures I mean."

"No, sir," the caretaker replied, but his wife was more expansive, she remembered and described vaguely a portrait that used to hang in the top bedroom that Maitland had now chosen as his own—the likeness of a young man she said it was, in old-fashioned clothes and holding a strange instrument.

IT WAS ASTONISHING how little light either the candles or the lamp gave in the large rooms; Maitland crossed the gallery carrying a single candle and found that he lit only shadows; even in his own, smaller room, the gentle flame was but a faint glow in the twilight. This did not trouble him; it would be long before it was dark and he was quite willing to sleep as soon as that came; the bed with the clean sheets and blankets, and the thick woollen curtains hooked up to the tester, looked comfortable; his own possessions, scattering out of the open valises, gave the room a homely look; he extinguished the candle and sat in the dusk, gazing out onto the field of poppies; when all colour else had gone from the scene, blended in one azure, the scarlet of these flowers burned through the twilight; over the landscape brooded, Maitland thought, an air of expectancy similar to that which filled the empty house. Surely some narcotic was really rising now from the poppies, he felt drowsy, as if with every breath he drew in oblivion.

At first the stillness was complete; Maitland considered with a quiet pleasure how far he was from any other human being—the lodge must be a quarter of a mile away; he was enclosed in the deserted park land and fields that belonged to Bothal.

There was a faint disturbance of the silence, a sound familiar to Maitland, yet one that at first he could not name, touched his ear—a gentle swishing, to and fro—was it a trail of creeper, eglantine or convolvulus tapping against a pane of glass?

No—Maitland listened and peered; ah, now he knew what the sound was, someone cutting grass, a man with a scythe.

The figure shaped itself out of the formless shadows that were gathering over the poppy fields; a man bending to a scythe cutting the thick, tall, flowered grass that grew at the edge of the poppies, now moving to the slow regular strokes, now pausing to draw the curved blade over the whetstone.

"How late he is," thought Maitland. "That must be the old gardener whom the caretaker spoke of—after all I suppose it is light enough for another hour—what a soothing sound it is—the swish of the scythe, how drowsy the scent of the poppies."

Maitland sighed, left his window and went downstairs—"the old fellow ought to be able to tell me quite a good deal about the place."

He left the house by one of the french windows that opened onto the back and stepped directly into the tangle of sun-dried grass that grew thickly round the brick wall; the sound of the scythe was louder in his ears but at first he could not see the mower and when he did discern him, on the verge of the poppy field, the old man seemed no more than the thickening of the shadows into a vague shape.

The scene was intangible and dim to Maitland, as if he had, he thought, returned from another world to visit this summer evening—a glimpse from his youth, long since lost.

"That is it," he whispered with some satisfaction, "forward to escape by death—backward to escape by dreams of a childhood that never was."

He approached the mower who did not look up from his task.

"You work very steadily," Maitland said to the stooping man. "It grows late."

The mower did not answer; the long swathes of grass fell at his feet and their perfume was stronger than that of the poppies; an echo cast back by the brick wall of the house gave the words—"it grows late."

Maitland turned away; feeling light-footed and drowsy, he passed round the poppy field, wandered through a grove of trees beyond and found himself in a meadow that dipped to a hollow.

In the hollow stood a small church

surrounded by a graveyard; Maitland supposed that it had once belonged to Bothal, but that now it served the scattered parish.

The grass grew thick over the graves; some dark grey crosses slanted forward and sideways; yew trees cast a dense shade; the moon floated above the squat Norman tower to which dark trails of ivy clung. Maitland stood in a vague meditation; he was thinking, not of his surroundings, but of the room waiting for him, the window open on the poppy field where the mower worked in silence, the bare neat house with its air of expectancy, the clean bed clothes piled beneath the faded curtains. He left the little graveyard and passed beyond the church where there was a piece of ground surrounded by a low wall of roughly shaped stones; in the far angle of this wall rose a tall, twisted thorn tree. The moonlight cast its crooked shadow across a solitary stone grave.

"Why," mused Maitland, "does he lie so lonely—away from all the others?" He vaulted the wall and stood by the long, worn stone, the shadow of the thorn now lay over his own body.

There was no name on the grave; deep into the dark stone was cut the rude semblance of a curious instrument, something like, Maitland thought, a pair of compasses with an odd attachment, set in a pentacle.

As he gazed at this he was aware that someone was standing close beside him, for he saw another shadow on the thick grass. He looked up and beheld a shabby stranger with a book under his arm.

"I see that you take an interest in the antiquities of this neighbourhood, sir."

Maitland, annoyed at the intrusion, replied dryly:

"Not any particular interest."

"This grave is, at least, interesting. You

know, of course, that this ground is not consecrated?"

"I guessed it. This is a suicide?"

"I don't know. He was one of the owners of Bothal—in fact, the last that lived there—they say—"

"Ah, the usual proviso!" smiled Maitland. "They say these old stories!"

"His name was John Maitland, you can see it in the church register."

Maitland still smiled; odd to stand over the grave of his namesake.

"He lived a hundred years ago and investigated the supernatural," said the stranger, moving beside the grave with a noiseless step. "I see that some weeds and thistles are growing here, a pity."

"Do you know any more of him?" asked Maitland; he too noticed tall plants that at first he had not observed, flags and spikes that the moonlight traced in dark shadows over the rough cutting of the instrument.

"He frequently tried to raise spirits," said the stranger, "and one night when he was drunk and goaded by a crowd of roisterers whom he had up at Bothal, he came here—to the churchyard and set his spells to raise the dead. He said he would have a bride from the grave. There was a girl buried here, she died two hundred years before—one of his own name, Joan Maitland. The fool said that he would have her or no other."

"Why fool?" asked Maitland. "It is delicious to be in love with the dead—yes, of all the manner of loving open to mankind that is, perhaps, the most beautiful."

"But the man was not content with dreams. He tried to bring back the dead. He invited Death to his house—to share his bed and board."

"And the invitation was accepted?" asked Maitland, watching the crooked shadow of a thorn that a light wind was waving to and fro across the rough stone of the grave.

"They treated it as a jest, of course, and they laughed very loudly when nothing happened after the incantation, but when they had returned to Bothal and were at their drink again one came to the door and beckoned Maitland away—they thought that she was one of his mortal fancies, for she seemed no more in her cotton frock and chaplet of wild flowers—he died that night and no one has since slept in Bothal and lived."

"So Death," smiled Maitland, "is the guest that the house is waiting for? 'Swept and garnished,' eh?"

"You may," said the stranger, "believe what you like."

Maitland felt suddenly fatigued; he sat down on the flat stone, and peering at it, perceived for the first time, that it bore his name along the rude cut of the unholy instrument, "John Maitland"—there was nothing else, not even a date.

Maitland looked up; the stranger had gone; had he ever been there?

"Where did I hear that story? In my own heart perhaps—yes, it seems to me that I invented it and that the stranger was but my other self."

He looked round at the church; it seemed small and insignificant, like an ancient shepherd, with his flock gathered around him—yes, the graves huddled close to the holy protection; Maitland thought of the church as full of prayers, hymns, tears and entreaties as a glass is filled with wine; but all this spiritual comfort and nourishment was shut away from him; he had seen the church doors, heavy, clamped with iron, barred against him; he was alone, outside, in the square of unconsecrated

ground with the shadow of the cursed, crooked thorn tree over him; the moon, rising higher, appeared smaller, like a ball of white fire thrown into the air—like a silver balloon that Maitland remembered launching into space when he was a child.

As he mused, gazing at the moon that reminded him of a childish toy, and seated on the grave that bore his name, he felt that past and present joined, and that escape by returning to his childhood and by death were resolved into one deliverance.

When he had been a little boy he had tried to sail his balloon to the moon that now itself seemed but a toy. The church, the tomb stones, the low wall, the thorn tree, all appeared now to the brooding man like phantoms evoked from his own brain, as if a sigh would demolish them, or a turn of his head change his dream.

He rose and looked around, peering

into the angles of the church that were darkened by shadows.

No, there was nothing there; the place was not haunted—like Bothal—it was empty, long since deserted.

He left the unhallowed ground and returned to the blessed plot where the dead who had died in the Lord slept under holy sod; he left the churchyard and came out into the meadow land; amid the grove of trees there seemed to be a pale shape, like an altar; he passed between the slim trunks, but there was nothing but a patch of moonlight in the centre of the trees; Maitland passed through to the meadow land beyond; he came up out of the hollow and could see Bothal standing clear and sharp in the moonlight, the gables distinct in every detail of bust and florid ornament and sway of fruit; silver lay over the poppy field, subduing the scarlet colour to the hue of a faint stain of dried blood; there were the dark outlines of the box hedges, the dense shape of the yew tree; Maitland was glad that he was going to sleep in that lonely house that night. He passed by the poppy field, he skirted the box hedges, he entered the french windows, found the candle where he had left it on the table by the bookcase and lit it with the matches in his pocket.

The clean-swept, handsome room seemed to have lost its air of expectancy, as if whoever the house had been waiting for had arrived; Maitland felt satisfied, as if he, too, had come home—to sleep.

He went upstairs, carefully guarding his gentle light with outspread hand; the paintings on the wall seemed to lengthen into vistas of scenes that he had once known and was now about to visit again—these lakes, these hills, these woods—these roads winding to the horizon.

As he reached the top of the house his sense of expectancy satisfied, increased; he was now sure that whoever the house was waiting for had arrived; he looked into the long gallery where the moonlight lay in squares on the sloping floor, then turned to his bedroom. "The mower has gone," he thought. "I did not see him yes, he has gone and no grass seemed to be cut."

On the threshold of his room stood a shadowy figure with wild flowers in her hair, a poppy coronal, surely, floating among her tresses. Maitland blew out his human light, entered his room, moving delicately among the shadows, lay down on his clean bed and slept.

ARJORIE BOWEN (1885–1952) was a prolific British author who wrote historical romances, supernatural horror, popular history, and biography.

ETH'S COMICS AND drawings have appeared in the *New York Times*, the *New Yorker*, the *Globe and Mail*, and countless other publications.

His latest graphic novel, *Clyde Fans*, won the prestigious Festival d'Angoulême's Prix Spécial du Jury.

He lives in Guelph, Ontario, with his wife, Tania, in an old house he has named "Inkwell's End."

Publisher's note: "The House by the Poppy Field" was first
published in *Kecksies and Other Twilight Tales*
by Arkham House in 1976.

Library and Archives Canada Cataloguing in Publication

Title: The house by the poppy field : a ghost story for
Christmas / Marjorie Bowen ; designed and
decorated by Seth.
Names: Bowen, Marjorie, 1888-1952, author. | Seth, 1962-
illustrator.
Description: Series statement: Seth's Christmas ghost stories
Identifiers: Canadiana 20230471420 | ISBN 9781771965736
(softcover)
Subjects: LCGFT: Short stories. | LCGFT: Ghost stories.
Classification: LCC PR6003.O676 H68 2023 | DDC
823/.912—dc23

Readied for the press by Daniel Wells
Illustrated and designed by Seth
Copyedited by Ashley Van Elswyk
Typeset by Vanessa Stauffer

PRINTED AND BOUND IN CANADA